Barney Beagle

WHAT IS AN EASY READER?

- This story has been carefully written to capture the interest of the young reader.

- It is told in a simple, direct style with a strong rhythm that adds enjoyment both to reading aloud and silent reading.

- Many key words are repeated regularly throughout the story. This skillful repetition helps the child to read independently. Encountering words again and again, the young reader practices the vocabulary he or she knows, and learns with ease the words that are new.

- Only 137 different words have been used, with plurals and root words counted once.

  More than one-half of the words in this story have been used at least three times.

  Almost one-third of the words in this story have been used at least seven times.

  Some words have been used from 19 to 33 times.

ABOUT THIS STORY

- Barney, the endearing Beagle who is the hero of this story, believes "every dog should have a boy," and waits for HIS boy impatiently. This dog-story-with-a-twist lends itself to discussion of animal-people relationships, and is a happy introduction for the younger reader to story-telling in the first person.

Barney Beagle

Story *by* JEAN BETHELL
Pictures *by* RUTH WOOD
Editorial Consultant: LILIAN MOORE

Wonder® Books

PRICE/STERN/SLOAN
Publishers, Inc., Los Angeles
1986

Introduction

Easy Readers help young readers discover what a delightful experience reading can be. The stories are such fun that they inspire children to try new reading skills. They are so easy to read that they provide encouragement and support for children as readers.

The adult will notice that the sentences aren't too long, the words aren't too hard, and the skillful repetition is like a helping hand. What the child will feel is: "This is a good story—and I can read it myself!"

For some children, the best way to meet these stories may be to hear them read aloud at first. Others, who are better prepared to read on their own, may need a little help in the beginning—help that is best given freely. Youngsters who have more experience in reading alone—whether in first or second or third grade—will have the immediate joy of reading "all by myself."

These books have been planned to help all young readers grow—in their pleasure in books and in their power to read them.

Lilian Moore
Specialist in Reading
Formerly of Division of Instructional Research,
New York City Board of Education

Copyright © 1962, 1981 by Price/Stern/Sloan Publishers, Inc.
Published by Price/Stern/Sloan Publishers, Inc.
410 North La Cienega Boulevard, Los Angeles, California 90048

ISBN: 0-8431-4301-0
Wonder® Books is a trademark of Price/Stern/Sloan Publishers, Inc.

How do you do?

My name is Barney Beagle.

I live in a pet shop.

These are my friends.

We have a pretty good time here.

I like the pet shop.

But I do not want to stay here.

I want to live in a house—

with a boy.

I am waiting for the right boy.

I hope he comes soon.

Here comes a boy now.

Is he MY boy?

I hope so.

No, he is Boxer's boy.
Anyone can see THAT.

The boy has to pay for Boxer.

Now he's taking Boxer home.

They look so happy.

Good-by, Boxer!

I wish MY boy would come.

Here comes someone!

Is it MY boy?

I hope so.

No, it's a girl.

She is Poodle's girl.

Anyone can see THAT.

The girl has to pay for Poodle.

Now she is taking Poodle home
with her.

How happy they look.

Good-by, Poodle!

I do hope MY boy comes soon.

Someone is coming now!

Maybe it's MY boy!

No, it's a man.

I think I know the dog he wants.

Yes, it's Sheepdog.

Anyone can see THAT.

The man has to pay for Sheepdog.

Now they are going home.

They do look happy.

Good-by, Sheepdog.

I wonder when MY boy will come?

Every day some boys and girls
come to the pet shop.

Every day some more dogs go home
with their boys and girls.
How happy they all look!

Where is MY boy?

Where can he be?

Today there are just two of us

in the pet shop.

Me, Barney Beagle,

and my friend Spot.

We are still waiting.

Here comes someone right now.

Here comes a boy!

Maybe, maybe, MAYBE

he is MY boy!

No, he is Spot's boy.

Anyone can see THAT.

The boy has to pay for Spot.

Now he is taking Spot home
with him.

They look so happy.

Good-by, Spot. Good-by.

Now all my friends are gone.

Now I am all alone.

It's no fun to be here all alone.

I wish MY boy would come.

Someone is coming now!

It's a boy!

Maybe—at last—

No, it is not MY boy.

Anyone can see THAT.

Stop that!

Go away!

Let go of me!

Stop that!

This boy wants me.

But I do not want him.

He wants to take me home.

But I will not go with him.

THERE!!

The boy is mad.

But I am glad.

I am glad to see him go.

But I do not like it here all alone.

I hope MY boy will come for me.

It is very late.

The man wants to go home.

I will be all alone tonight.

I guess MY boy will never come.

Someone is coming!

I do not want to look.

Maybe, maybe, MAYBE....

It IS a boy!

It is MY boy!

Anyone can see THAT.

I'm so happy to see you!

You took so long to come!

Now he has to pay for me.

Then he will take me home.

Let's go. Let's go.

Come on! Come on!

Why don't we go home?

The man is looking at the money.

"You need more money," he tells

my boy.

My boy looks very sad.

"That is all the money I have,"

he says.

He cannot pay for me!

He cannot take me home!

"Please?" says my boy.

"He's a very small dog."

The man looks at me.

He looks at my boy.

He thinks and thinks and thinks.

Then he laughs.

"Yes," he says. "Barney is
a very small dog.
And I do want to sell him
before I go home.
Yes, you can have him."

Hooray! Hooray!

I have my boy at last!

"Come on, Barney," says my boy.

"Let's go home."

Good-by, pet shop.

Good-by, pet shop man.

I'm going home with MY boy!

I think every dog should have
a boy.
Don't you?